Rob Scotton

Russell

the Sheep

HarperCollins *Publishers*

Special thanks to Maria and Sue for helping to
make Russell the sheep he is today!

—R.S.

Russell the Sheep
Copyright © 2005 by Rob Scotton
Manufactured in China

HarperCollins Children's Books,
a division of HarperCollins Publishers,
1350 Avenue of the Americas, New York, NY 10019.
www.harperchildrens.com

Library of Congress Cataloging-in-Publication Data

Scotton, Rob.
Russell the sheep / by Rob Scotton.— 1st ed.
p. cm.
Summary: Russell the sheep tries all different ways to get to sleep.
ISBN 0-06-059848-4 — ISBN 0-06-059849-2 (lib. bdg.)
[1. Bedtime—Fiction. 2. Sheep—Fiction. 3. Sleep—Fiction. 4. Counting—
Fiction.] I. Title.
PZ7.S4354Ru 2005   2005024274
[E]—dc22   CIP
                                                                              AC

Typography by Martha Rago
1 2 3 4 5 6 7 8 9 10
❖
First Edition

This book is dedicated to
Mum, Dad, Nan, and Liz,
with my love and the biggest thank you.

—R.S.

Russell the sheep lived in Frogsbottom Field.

At the end of a long busy day....

night fell and the sheep got ready for bed.

Soon all was quiet.

Except for…

Russell.

No matter how hard he tried, Russell could not fall asleep.

But the really dark
really scared him.

"Maybe if it were
really dark," he
thought, "I'd be
able to sleep."

"Perhaps I'm too hot," he thought.

"Perhaps I'm not."

Russell pulled up a pillow…

but the pillow hopped away…

hopping mad!

"Maybe I need a better place to sleep," he decided, and went for a walk.

Russell spied the trunk of the rusty car.

It was **too** cramped!

He tried the hollow of a tree.

That was **too creepy!**

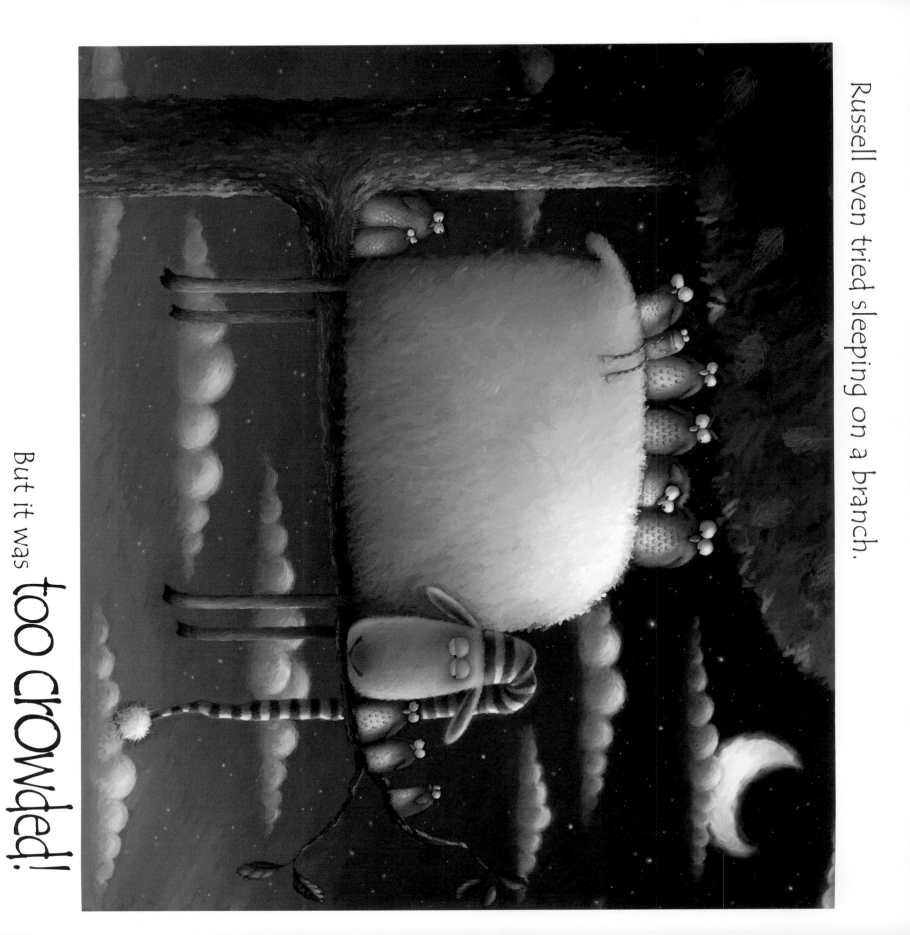

Russell even tried sleeping on a branch.

But it was too crowded!

WHAT'S A SHEEP TO DO?

Russell thought he would never get to sleep. But then he had a brilliant idea.

What if he tried to count things? That would make him fall asleep.

Russell counted his feet.

One....

two....

three....

four.

Not tired.

"Hmmm. I guess I need more feet," he decided.

"What next?"

The stars! Russell counted each and every one.

One...two...three...four...five...

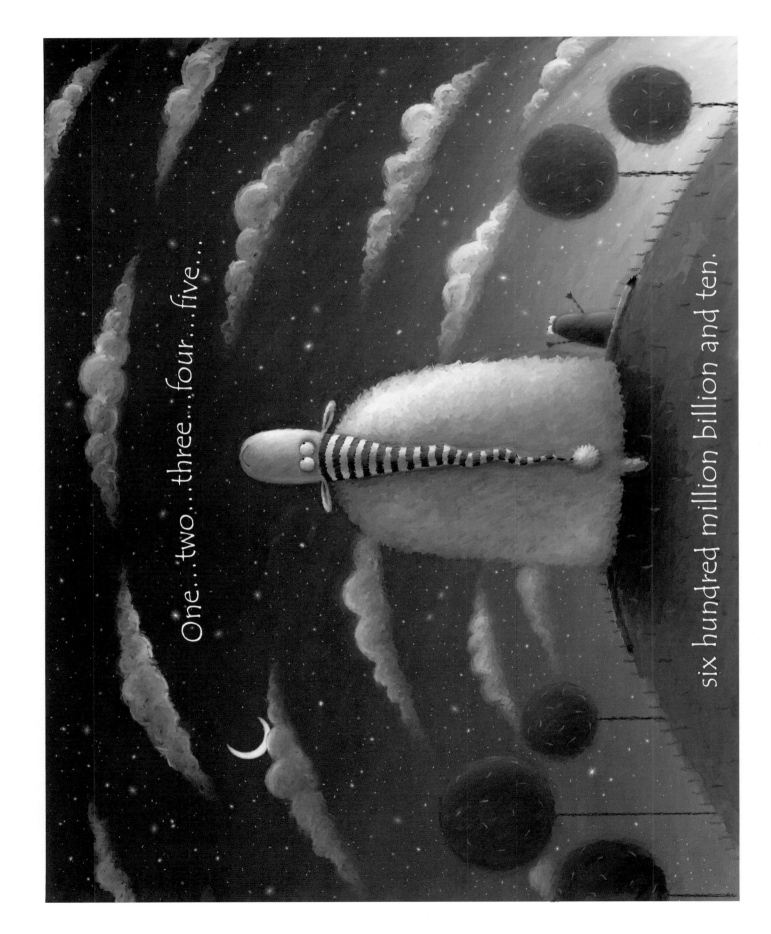

six hundred million billion and ten.

And Russell was wide awake!

He counted them again . . .

six hundred million billion and ten!

And still wide awake!

Russell thought very hard.

In fact, he thought so hard, his hat went ziggy-zaggy!

"I know," he shouted. "I'll count sheep!"

One…

two…

three…four…five…

six….

nine...

seven...eight...

"Still awake," he said and sighed.

Then Russell realized he had forgotten
to count one very important little sheep...

"Ten!"

...himself!

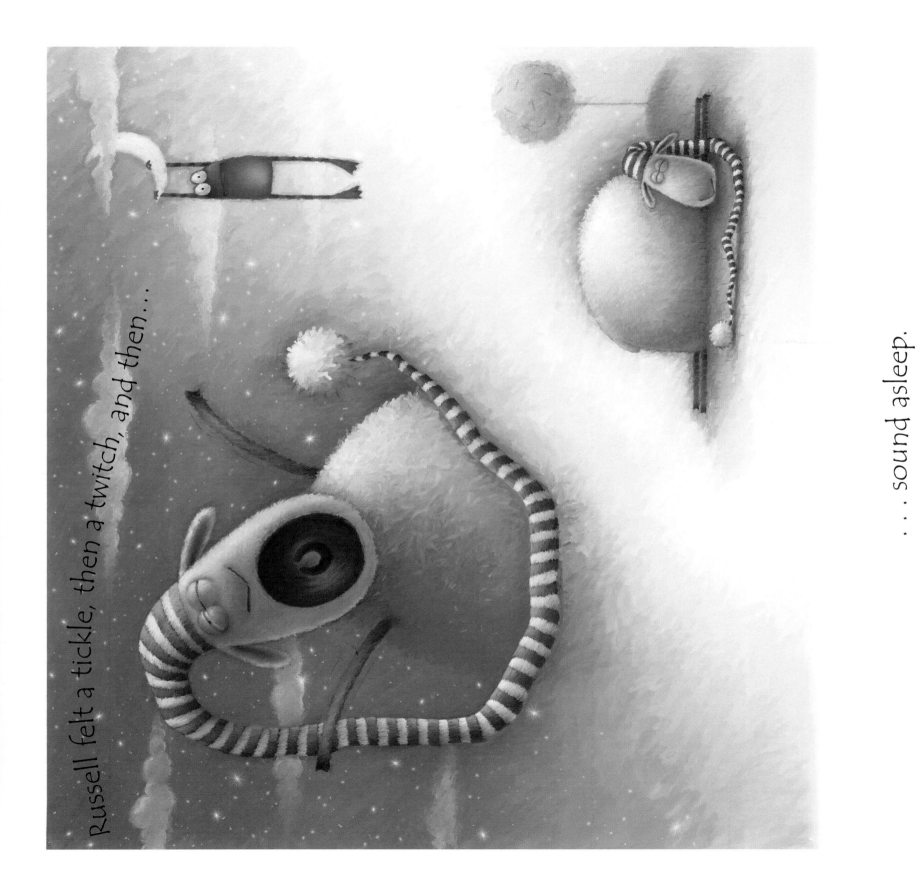

Russell felt a tickle, then a twitch, and then...

...sound asleep.

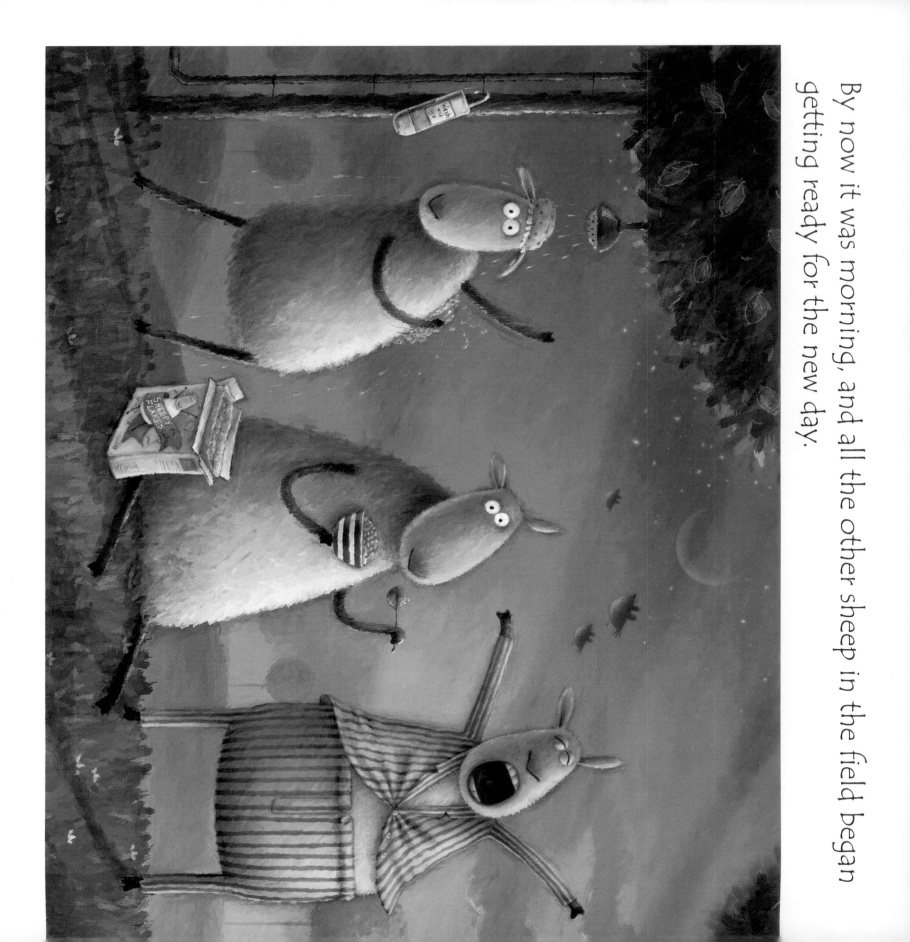

By now it was morning, and all the other sheep in the field began getting ready for the new day.

Soon everyone was up. Everyone that is, except for . . .

Russell.